New Jersey

ATLANTIC OCEAN

N

Kate Heads West

by Pat Brisson

illustrations by Rick Brown

Simon & Schuster Books for Young Readers

Text copyright © 1990 by Pat Brisson
Illustrations copyright © 1990 by Rick Brown

SIMON & SCHUSTER BOOKS FOR YOUNG READERS
An imprint of Simon & Schuster Children's Publishing Division
1230 Avenue of the Americas
New York, New York 10020
Simon & Schuster Books for Young Readers is a trademark of Simon & Schuster
Printed and bound in Hong Kong by South China Printing Company (1988) Ltd.
10 9 8 7 6 5 4 3 2

The text of this book is set in ITC Veljovic.
Book design by Julie Quan

LIBRARY OF CONGRESS CATALOGING-IN-PUBLICATION DATA
Brisson, Pat.
   Kate heads west / by Pat Brisson; illustrations by Rick Brown.
—1st American ed.   p.   cm.
   Summary: In a series of letters to her relatives and friends, Kate
describes her trip through Oklahoma, Texas, New Mexico, and Arizona
with her best friend, Lucy, and Lucy's parents.
   [1. West (U.S.)—Fiction.   2. Voyages and travels—Fiction.
3. Letters.]   I. Brown, Rick, date. ill.   II. Title.
PZ7.B78046On   1990 [E]—dc20
89-27590   CIP   AC
ISBN 0-02-714345-7

For my husband, Emil,
and for our sons,
Gabriel, Noah, Benjamin,
and Zachary — my favorite
traveling companions

— P.B.

For Michael, Timmy,
and Abigail

— R.B.

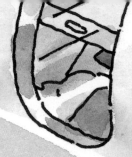

August 1, Sky Above You, U.S.A.

Dear Mom and Dad,

    Look! Up in the sky! It's a bird! It's a plane! It's me—Kate!

    Lucy and I decided to write letters before we land in Oklahoma City. Lucy's mom is taking a nap, and her dad is reading about the Hopi Indians. Thanks a *lot* for letting me go on vacation with the Toopers.

    We're up so high it hardly feels like we're moving. And guess what—we got to see the Mississippi River!

    Our pilot is Captain Sara Maleski, and after she told us our altitude and stuff over the intercom, Lucy said, "Let's be pilots when we grow up, Kate." I said, "But we'd never see each other because we'd be flying all over the world." And Lucy said, "But we could always meet for lunch in Cairo or Paris or Honolulu."

    I told the flight attendant about our plan, and she said she'd take us up to the cockpit to meet Captain Maleski after we land. Yippee!

                      Your favorite daughter,
                        Kate

P.S. Mr. Tooper is renting a car at the airport. Lucy and I are hoping for a red convertible.

John Wayne's Hat

KACHINA DOLL

State Flower Mistletoe

SPURS

August 2, Oklahoma City, Oklahoma

Dear Brian,

Today we went to the National Cowboy Hall of Fame. One part of it was like an old Western town. It had a jail, a gold mine, a telegraph office, a stagecoach, and a sod house (which means that the roof is made of chunks of ground with grass still growing on them).

There was a whole bunch of stuff that belonged to John Wayne. I liked the kachina dolls best.

And there was even a rodeo bull named Tornado and two bucking broncs named Midnight and Five Minutes to Midnight buried in the garden.

It's three o'clock in the morning, and I'm writing to you from the tree house in Lucy's cousin's backyard. Her name is Tara, and she has a cat named Lucky Eddy, who only has one ear.

Are you taking good care of Buster and Bruno? Don't you dare give them any potato chips—just two shakes of fish food, Brian, and that's all.

Your favorite sister,
Kate

P.S. Mr. T. rented a yellow station wagon and Lucy and I sit in the way back and make funny faces at the truck drivers.

August 3, Oklahoma City, Oklahoma

O-Si-Yo, Mrs. Snyder (that's Cherokee for "hello"),

We were thinking about you yesterday at a place in Tahlequah called the Cherokee Heritage Center. There's a whole village just like a Cherokee village from three hundred years ago. People were making arrowheads and pottery and baskets and beadwork and even a dugout canoe. Remember how our social studies books said the Cherokee built fires in the logs to clean out the insides? They really do—we saw it!

Mr. Tooper knows all about the Native Americans because he's a history teacher. Anyway, he said in 1838–1839 the Cherokee were forced to leave their homes in Georgia and North Carolina in the middle of the winter. Lots of people—even kids and little babies—died on the trip. We saw a play about it called *The Trail of Tears.*

This would have been a great field trip for our class, Mrs. Snyder. Too bad Oklahoma is about a thousand miles away from New Jersey.

Your favorite students,
Kate and Lucy

State Tree
American Redbud

Miles of Sunflowers ←

August 4, Oklahoma City, Oklahoma

Dear Dr. Taverna (World's Best Dentist),

I went to the World Championship Watermelon Seed Spitting Contest today in Weatherford, and I thought of you because you're the only other person who ever wanted me to spit. You'd love this place. Everybody spits here, from little kids who can hardly walk, all the way up to old people (called smooth mouths because they can take out their false teeth).

The world record is 57′8½″. I practiced for a long time, but the best I could do was 15′2¼″.

See you in September!

Your favorite patient,
Kate

state
Bird

Scissor-tailed
Flycatcher

WORLD CHAMPIONSHIP
WATERMELON SEED
SPITTING CONTEST

67

State
Flower
Bluebonnet

August 6, Fort Worth, Texas

Dear Buster and Bruno,

I hope Brian's keeping your bowl nice and clean like he promised me he would. If he threatens to flush you down the toilet, tell him I won't give him the genuine cowboy hat I bought for him at the rodeo last night in Fort Worth.

My favorite part of the rodeo was the cowgirls racing their horses around barrels in big figure eights. They went around the corners so fast it looked like the horses would fall right over. Lucy and I would probably be world champion barrel-racers if we lived in Texas and owned horses.

Yesterday afternoon we went to a Japanese garden. It was very quiet and peaceful there. Lucy's mom told us the Meditation Garden is just like one she's been to at a temple in Kyoto, Japan. She said it's nice to find a little bit of Japan in Texas. And there were beautiful imperial carp swimming in the pools there which reminded me of you.

Your favorite owner,
Kate

P.S. Tell Mom and Dad not to worry — I'm being really polite.

Imperial
Carp

Japanese
Garden

August 9, Houston, Texas

Dear Bucko,

   Greetings from Johnson Space Center! Did you know that astronauts have brought eight hundred pounds of moon rocks back to earth? We tried to get some for you, but they said they're not for sale.

   We saw rockets, lunar modules, and simulators, where astronauts get ready for going into space, and a bunch of other space stuff. We didn't see any astronauts, though. I told our guide at Mission Control that Lucy wants to be an aeronautical engineer when she grows up, and she let Lucy say "Discovery? This is Mission Control. Come in, please" over the microphone.

   We both chipped in and bought you this neat anti-gravity pen so when you finally get to be an astronaut you'll be able to write us letters from Mars.

   Isn't it nice to know your friends are always thinking of you?

                    Over and out,
                    Kate & Lucy

P.S. We're staying at the Satellite Motel. It's so great. There's a soda machine right down the hall from us and an ice machine with free ice cubes!

APOLLO II

State tree, Pecan

offshore oil rig

sea turtle

August 11, Corpus Christi, Texas

Dear Aunt Ginny and Uncle Bill,

Surprise! It's me—Kate! I'm in Corpus Christi with my best friend, Lucy, and her parents.

Yesterday we rented a jeep and drove out to Padre Island National Seashore. The ride was really bumpy—without seat belts we would have bounced right onto the floor. But the beach was beautiful and the sky was so blue. We flew kites and hunted for shells and I shouted hello to you across the Gulf of Mexico. Did you hear me in Tallahassee?

Today we went on a fishing boat called the *Bluebonnet*. Lucy's parents caught three spotted seatrout. Lucy and I didn't catch anything, but we did see *seven* dolphins and a Portuguese man-of-war!

Your favorite niece,
Kate

The
Alamo →

August 13, On the Road

Dear Mom and Dad,

We're on the longest drive of the vacation — 480 miles from San Antonio to Carlsbad, New Mexico.

Lucy and I sang "The Stars at Night Are Big and Bright, Deep in the Heart of Texas" for the first 100 miles. But then Mrs. T. asked us to do something quiet like count cactus plants. We only got up to sixty-seven.

Then Lucy's dad said we should stop and stretch our legs. Opening the car door was like opening an oven door. My face started baking as soon as I got out. But the air smelled beautiful, not quite like flowers but just as nice.

I thought the desert would be completely empty except for sand. But there are lots of plants, and I saw some birds (but no roadrunners), and two rabbits with the longest ears I've ever seen, and four lizards and some bugs. I was hoping we'd see a scorpion or a tarantula, but we weren't that lucky.

Your favorite daughter,
Kate

P.S. Hey, Brian, remember Davy Crockett and the battle at the Alamo? We went there yesterday. It looked a lot bigger on TV.

August 15, Carlsbad, New Mexico

Dear Bucko,

Hello from the Carlsbad Caverns! You should see this place, Bucko. It's like something from another planet! It took us almost two hours just to get down to the Big Room (which is *really* big—almost the size of fourteen football fields). There's even a little lunchroom down there, so we had some burritos.

But the best part is this: In the evening about a zillion bats fly out to go hunting for bugs to eat. The sound of all those bat wings flapping and all those little high-pitched bat squeaks gave us goose bumps. We sat outside the caves, far enough away so they wouldn't think *we* were dinner, even though Mr. T. kept reminding us that bats eat bugs, not people. They'll hunt all night long and fly back in the morning. We'll be on our way to El Paso by then.

It is so CREEPY—we know you would just *love* it here!

Your bat friends,
Kate & Lucy

state tree
piñon pine
(common nut pine)

state
bird
Mockingbird

August 17, El Paso, Texas

Buenos Días, Aunt Mag (that's Spanish for "good day"),
     I'm on vacation in Texas with my friend Lucy and guess what—we *walked* to Mexico yesterday! (We walked from El Paso across the Rio Grande to Juarez.) It was my first time in another country and it was great! I spent the money you gave me on a beautiful skirt, which comes down to my feet, and a blouse with little flowers embroidered all over it. *Muchas gracias!* (That means "thank you very much.")
     I wore them both to the Ballet Folklorico last night. I expected it to be like the *Nutcracker,* but it was a lot faster and more exciting. The costumes were all bright colors, and the women's wide skirts swirled around them when they danced. It was *excelente*! Lucy and I have been practicing in the hotel room—she bought a skirt, too. We decided we're going to be dancers when we grow up.

                    Your favorite niece,
                    Kate

P.S. Here's some more Spanish that I learned: *Dispensame* means "excuse me" and *¡yo quiero a Mexico!* means "I love Mexico!"

chili
Peppers →

Natural
Arches →

State Flower
Yucca

August 18, Buckhorn, New Mexico

Dear Mrs. Heath,

How are things at the library? We visited the Gila Cliff Dwellings National Monument today. We had to climb a narrow trail to get there, and one spot was perfect for hearing your echo from the opposite wall of the canyon. Lucy and I yelled our names to see how many echoes we could get back. (Lucy got six, but I got seven.)

Anyway, the cliff dwellings are stone buildings built right into the side of the cliff. They are about a thousand years old! The Mogollon Indians built them for protection from other tribes. I guess it worked, because they lived here for hundreds of years.

Your favorite reader,
Kate

August 21, Ramah, New Mexico

Dear Mom and Dad,

We visited El Morro National Monument today. It's called the Inscription Rock because Spanish explorers and other people traveling west carved their names in it hundreds of years ago when they stopped here for water. Some people even wrote poems or told about great things they had done. It's about two hundred feet high, so it was easy to find.

The park ranger said that nobody's allowed to carve on El Morro anymore, but said we could write something on the rock in front of the Visitors' Center. So we borrowed a nail file from Lucy's mom and wrote: LUCY + KATE — FRIENDS TO THE END.

It was slow work, but now we'll be there for a hundred years at least.

Your favorite daughter,
Kate

P.S. We've gone 3,109 miles! From New Jersey to Oklahoma City was 1,000. From Oklahoma City to Corpus Christi was 1,067, and from there to here was 1,042.

State Bird
Roadrunner
→

Petroglyph →

August 23, the Petrified Forest, Arizona

Dear Brian,

We are having the *best* time! Today we went to the Petrified Forest. It wasn't like I expected, but it was still great. I thought there would be all these trees standing around looking like concrete. But there aren't that many trees at all and actually, they're lying around like logs. They look like marbles all melted together — swirls of red and yellow and purple and pink.

I took some great pictures of the petroglyphs (old rock carvings made by the Anasazi Indians). My favorite is a mountain lion with his claws bared and his mouth open in a terrible snarl.

Tomorrow we're going to see the Hopi Snake Dance. Mr. T. said the Hopi dance with live rattlesnakes in their mouths without getting bit. We are also going to visit a pueblo built on a mesa. Mesas are hills with steep sides and flat tops, almost like tables.

Aren't you glad you're my little brother? There's *so* much you can learn from me.

Your favorite sister,
Kate

State Flower
Saguaro Cactus

Mesas

pueblos

Grand Canyon → Awesome!

August 28, Grand Canyon, Arizona

Dear Mom and Dad,

Thank you, thank you, thank you for letting me come on this trip with Lucy! I can't believe I'll be home in less than a week. We're spending these last days at the Grand Canyon before we fly back. I think they should have named it the Stupendously Gigantic Canyon because it is so unbelievably big. In some places the river is a *mile* down from were we stand— I've even seen birds flying below me. At one lookout point we looked down and saw clouds. Lucy said it was fog, but I think it's the same thing.

We learned so much here that the park ranger gave us Official Junior Ranger Badges!

Yesterday we went river rafting in another canyon. Lucy and I screamed almost the entire trip, and Mr. T. said he had to give our guide a really big tip because we probably broke his eardrums.

Your favorite daughter,
Kate

State Bird
Cactus
Wren

September 4, Phillipsburg, New Jersey

Dear Mr. and Mrs. Tooper,

     Thanks for taking me on vacation with you. I had a great time. The things I liked best were walking to Mexico, the raft ride down the Colorado River, and the cowgirls at the rodeo.

     I learned a lot about Oklahoma cowboys, Texas deserts, New Mexico bats, and Arizona Indians. But the best thing I learned was how lucky Lucy is to have you for parents and how lucky I am to be

                      Lucy's best friend,
                      Kate

P.S. I want you to know I wrote this thank-you note even before my mother told me to.